Dear Parent:

Your child's love of reading starts here!

Every child learns to read in a different way and at his or her own speed. Some go back and forth between reading levels and read favorite books again and again. Others read through each level in order. You can help your young reader improve and become more confident by encouraging his or her own interests and abilities. From books your child reads with you to the first books he or she reads alone, there are I Can Read Books for every stage of reading:

SHARED READING
Basic language, word repetition, and whimsical illustrations, ideal for sharing with your emergent reader

BEGINNING READING
Short sentences, familiar words, and simple concepts for children eager to read on their own

READING WITH HELP
Engaging stories, longer sentences, and language play for developing readers

READING ALONE
Complex plots, challenging vocabulary, and high-interest topics for the independent reader

I Can Read Books have introduced children to the joy of reading since 1957. Featuring award-winning authors and illustrators and a fabulous cast of beloved characters, I Can Read Books set the standard for beginning readers.

A lifetime of discovery begins with the magical words **"I Can Read!"**

Visit www.icanread.com for information
on enriching your child's reading experience.

I Can Read® and I Can Read Book® are trademarks of HarperCollins Publishers.

The Adventures of Paddington: Pancake Day!

Based on the Paddington novels written and created by Michael Bond
PADDINGTON™ and PADDINGTON BEAR™ © Paddington and Company/Studiocanal S.A.S. 2020
Paddington Bear™, Paddington™, and PB™ are trademarks of Paddington and Company Limited
Licensed on behalf of Studiocanal S.A.S. by Copyrights Group
www.paddington.com

ISBN 978-0-06-298304-6 (trade bdg.)—ISBN 978-0-06-298303-9 (pbk.)

20 21 22 23 24 LSCC 10 9 8 7 6 5 4 3 2 1 ❖ First Edition

My First

I Can Read!

The Adventures of

Paddington™

Pancake Day!

Based on the episode "Paddington Makes Pancakes"

by Jon Foster and James Lamont

Adapted by Alyssa Satin Capucilli

HARPER

An Imprint of HarperCollinsPublishers

In this story you will meet:

Paddington: He loves his aunt Lucy and writes her lots of letters. He also loves sweet orange jam called marmalade.

the Brown Family: Mr. and Mrs. Brown, Judy, and Jonathan love having a bear at home.

Mrs. Bird: She looks after the Brown family. She cooks the very best treats.

Dear Aunt Lucy,
Today is Pancake Day!
Mrs. Bird will make flat,
sweet cakes for all . . .

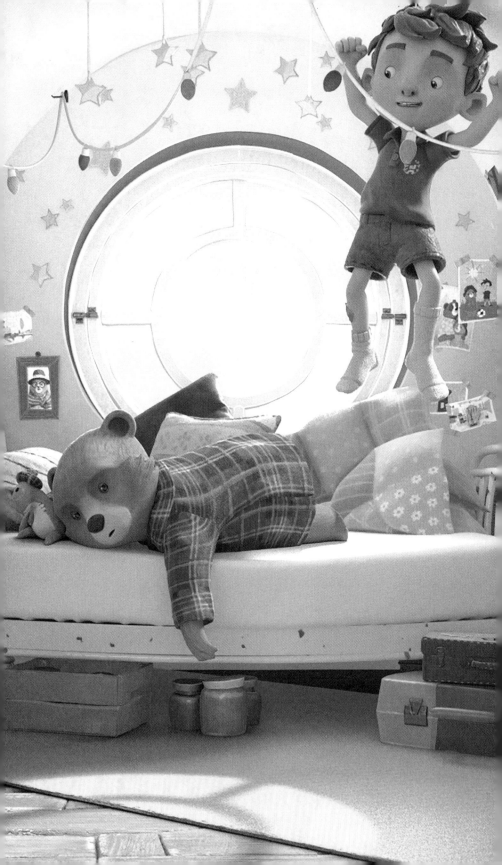

It was Pancake Day!
Jonathan was so excited
that he woke up Paddington.

Paddington was excited, too.
He wanted to try
his first pancake!

Paddington wanted pancakes
with marmalade.
He loved marmalade!

Everyone ran to the kitchen.

Paddington looked at the table.

No pancakes.

Paddington looked at the stove.

No pancakes.

Then Paddington saw Mrs. Bird.

"I'm sorry, wee bear," she said.

"I had a little accident.

I cannot make pancakes today."

No pancakes on Pancake Day?
The Brown family was very sad.

Paddington wanted to help.

He saw a pan.

Paddington saw a tall cake.

But the pan-cake was not flat.

Paddington knew what to do.

He jumped!

Splat!

"I did it!

A flat pancake!"

Now the pancake was stuck!
Paddington tugged.

He tugged again.

The pancake hit Paddington!

Making pancakes was hard!

Paddington saw a bowl.

He saw milk.

Suddenly—CRASH!
A book fell on his head.
"This book will help!"

"One egg, two eggs,
three eggs,"
said Paddington.

"Oops!" said Paddington.

Paddington mixed the batter.
Mixing was tricky.

Paddington tossed the pancake.

It went up, and it fell down.

Oh no! Not again!

Plop!

"I'm sorry, Mrs. Bird.
I tried to make pancakes
for Pancake Day."

"But all I made is a mess!"
said Paddington.

"Maybe I can help, wee bear,"
said Mrs. Bird.

Paddington and Mrs. Bird
got to work.

Sniff! Sniff!

The smell of pancakes
filled the air!

"Happy Pancake Day,"
said Paddington.

It was the best Pancake Day ever.

It takes a good friend
to make pancakes, Aunt Lucy.
And marmalade!

 Love from Paddington